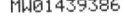

DISPLACED

Dreams of home town life are shattered by the plant closing.

Displaced is Copyright protected © 2022 by John E. Davis. All Rights Reserved.

All rights reserved. No part of this book may be reproduced in any form or by any electronic or mechanical means including information storage and retrieval systems, without permission in writing from the author. The only exception is by a reviewer, who may quote short excerpts in a review.

Cover designed by Cover Designer

This book is a work of fiction. Names, characters, places, and incidents either are products of the author's imagination or are used fictitiously. Any resemblance to actual persons, living or dead, events, or locales is entirely coincidental.

John E. Davis
Visit my website at www.AuthorName.com

Printed in the United States of America

First Printing: July 30th, 2022
Kindle Direct Publishing

ISBN: 9798842205431

Table of Contents

The Awakening 4
The Search 7
Dreams in the Rearview Mirror 10
Kindness without Speaking 14
The Pay Line 17
Something's wrong 19
The Next Day 22
A New Start 25
Moving on 27
Honcho Leaves 32
Thrust into the Unknown 34
Recovery 39
A Glimmer of Hope 41
The End 42

THE AWAKENING

I try again to start the engine alone with a prayer. "Please, God, let this nightmare be only a dream." The courage-draining proof comes all too quickly. The answer from under the hood is a hideous clicking. Even after I remove the key, the sound reverberates in my head. Is this like what a blindfolded prisoner hears just before the executioner shoots?

An amber halo surrounds a glorious desert sunrise. My anxiety lifts as the daylight pushes the blackness of night aside. Its healing warmth feels good on my face as I unfold from the driver's seat, where I dozed off only two hours ago. I still can't believe how we got into this mess. My slender wife Millie is scrunched into the seat next to me. Our son Bobby and his grandmother are both asleep behind us in the back seat.

As I open the door to step onto the gravel road, my aching neck and shoulders remind me of everything I tried to do to get this retired Checker taxi going again. Rubbing my eyes brings back the reality that nothing I tried worked; though I did my best, the engine is dead. I should have known this could happen. We left everything except for a few clothes and some food back in Tucson. We hoped to make the food last until we found work, but now we are down to a plastic jug of water, three oranges, and a box of Animal Crackers. The torment from searching for weeks to find work tightens in my chest, but I must move on.

The only chance for our survival is to concentrate on positive thoughts and focus on finding a way to keep everyone safe. My desire is strong, but my energy is sucked away by an immense anxiety attack. Fear of failing my family tugs at my arms and torso like sandbags pulling me down.

I force my feet to take me away as I try to rescue my mind from despair. A gurgle releases a reflux belch burning in my throat as I lead forward to stretch. Hopefully, stretching will help to quiet the nagging discomfort. Rolling my head loosens the tension in my shoulders. The shadow of a slow circling hawk floats over the road in front of me. I envy the freedom of this lone bird drifting high above me in the blue.

"Be careful out there, dear...there might be snakes." Millie steps from the taxi as she brushes her hair away from her face.

"Is Bobby awake?" I motion for her to join me so we can witness the sun rising together.

"Not yet." Her index finger placed against her lips signals for me to speak softer. She glides toward me, gathering her skirt in one hand while holding her hair back with the other. Her expression alternates from pain to smile as she tiptoes barefoot across the gravel. Sunbeams reach for the shadows racing westward over the desert's floor. Native amber, terra cotta, and blue sky come alive as the musty smell of night surrenders to the warmth.

"Did you sleep?" she asks.

"A little, how about you?" Holding her body next to mine is soothing.

"Yeah. Had a dream about the ocean." Millie nudges me with her elbow as she points into the distance. "What is that patch of green over there?"

"Thank God." I squeeze her hand. "There must be people there and I'll go to get help."

"Do you want us to go too?"

"It is safer to stay here. I'll make a tent."

"What will I do with a tent?" Millie tilts her head as laughter spews.

"I may be awhile, and you guys will need a place to keep out of the sun."

We return to the taxi, where I pull a roll of duct tape from the glove box and fasten our blanket above the open doors. "You should be okay under this. I'll bring back help as soon as I can."

Millie kisses me. "Don't worry so much." She slips a half-full water bottle into my back pocket. "We'll all be fine." The sparkle in her almond eyes gives me faith that she is telling the truth and that everything will somehow work out.

"Wait, you forgot something." She waves for me to look into the back seat. "He needs a hug before you go." Hugging my six-year-old son reminds me how important it is to be strong.

"Hey Buddy. I'm going to that green patch to get some help. Okay?"

"I wanna go too," he bounces on the seat.

"I know, son, but you gotta stay here to take care of Mommy." His lower lip quivers as tears well in his eyes - my heart breaks as I turn away. Millie picks him up and signals for me to leave.

THE SEARCH

Distant blue-grey mountains flank the right side of the road with flat scrubland with prickly bushes on my left. Leaving my family alone in this place gives me a rush of uneasiness. Millie tells me not to worry, but what if she's wrong?

Anger hammers at me when I think about the plant closing back home and foreigners taking over our jobs. "It's not fair!" I throw a stone as far as I can while yelling to the sky.

An hour later, I stand in amazement in front of a fence surrounding a field of lush leaves of sugar beets planted in rows. "How can this field be so alive in such a barren place?" A weathered irrigation pump-house, hissing and sputtering, comes to life as sprinkler heads gush with water overhead. Farther away, workers wearing straw hats unload baskets from trucks.

I spy an old truck holding up a help-wanted sign in the corner of the field. Its tires and glass are gone. Even the paint has given itself away to the wind. Gnawing in my stomach reminds me: my most pressing need is to raise enough money to buy food and get help. Faith nourished my courage and sustained my will until three miles ago. That vision vanished along with my confidence when the car broke down.

I push the gate open and walk toward flatbed trucks parked by a barn. I follow the smell of cigarette smoke, looking for someone in charge.

"Hello, anyone here?" I hear a deep grunt from a man dozing in a chair in the shade of the old metal barn.

"The sign out front says you need help." The large man squints, looks at me from head to toe, and shakes his head no. My pulse pounds and my jaw tightens. He looks like one of them who took over the plant and moved our jobs.

"I can work," I say. "All I'm asking is for a chance to show you--" He interrupts me waving his hands, "No hablo ingles." The name above his shirt pocket spells, "Honcho."

"Please, my car broke down, and my family needs food." As if irritated by my insistence, he stands up, adjusts his straw hat, and flips a basket to me; I catch it one handed. He noticed my determination and motions for me to follow his lead into the field of workers.

The sun is high as he stops to remove his hat and wipe sweat from his chiseled brow. A sparkle reflects off a gold tooth as he puts a cigarette to his lips. He glances back at me as he strikes a match against his silver belt buckle and motions for me to move the basket. Cigarette smoke in the still air lazily rises into his squinting eyes.

Honcho, with a handful of coarse green-top and a manly grunt, swings the beet, now untethered from Mother Earth, into the basket. He takes a drag from his cigarette, points to a green top, and nods for me to try. I bend low to grab a handful of leaves, give them a yank, but the plant fights back. Honcho's grin widens as the beet confirms its will to remain in place. I dust myself off and center my body over the plant, grab it with a new level of determination, and whisper, "Only one of us is going to survive this."

Its roots make a cracking sound as the beet surrenders. A rush of excitement surges as I drop it into the basket; however, the victory feels hollow. I am sad for displacing this living thing. I understand the desire to stay connected to one's roots--I was uprooted when the factory back home closed.

A hand touching my shoulder startles me back to the task. Honcho stands beside me, pointing at the beets. As I grab the next victim, he takes a long puff on his cigarette, shakes his head, and strides back to his chair in the shade.

I reach for another beet top when my thoughts collide with reality. We are stranded, and the only protection from the desert sun is an awning made from our wedding blanket. A broken-down taxi out there is my harvest basket. "How did it go so wrong?" Tears of regret fall as I continue to think of happier thoughts from back home.

Who am I trying to kid? We had to leave Tennessee. Foreigners shut down the plant and took our jobs south. The whole town was out of work. We are here because our retired taxi was the only transportation we could afford. Millie's brother found it at Alvin's salvage yard near the crusher. 'Old 201' was pretty much intact except for needing a carburetor, tires, and a battery. I traded my shotgun for the tires off Curt's double-wide. We scrounged parts from other junkers to get it on the road again. Family teamwork and a trip through Benny's Land-o-Suds gave the old taxi enough dignity for people to signal us for hire. We were confident having transportation that we could survive on Mom's disability checks until we found work elsewhere.

DREAMS IN THE REARVIEW MIRROR

The end of my row is now in sight. A lizard slithers ahead of me as other workers return for baskets. I better hurry up, or I'll look bad. Squatting as I yank lets me use my upper body to help lever the plants. As soon as my basket is full, another worker signals me to hand it over and then tosses me an empty one. In this heat, the minutes tick slowly into hours.

The memory of the night in Tucson pops into my head out of nowhere. That night we decided to change Checker's identity. I remember buying the spray cans of K-Mart green outdoor furniture paint. Old 201 "officially" retired from its taxi uniform at 9:30 PM that night. We celebrated with a liter of cola behind the dumpster near the lawn and garden section. It took almost two hours to paint it, and other than a few runs on the driver's door and the lumps on the top from over-curious bugs, the new paint looked good. Old 201 took on an entirely new image. Sure, it still had the shape of a Checker taxi, with its oversized everything, but it was no longer that bright yellow with its checkerboard stripe that caused bystanders to gawk at us.

Laughing voices around me bring me back to reality picking beets. The seam on the back of my T-shirt rubs against me like the jagged edge of a hacksaw blade. An older worker trades me an empty basket for the full one I dragged to the end of the row. I give him a polite head bob as he points for me to change direction to harvest a row back toward the barn. The leaves in this row are damp, and the heavenly mist from the sprinkler heads occasionally floats over me. My thoughts wander as my weary body stumbles forward, harvesting one beet at a time.

I straighten up to stretch my aching back and hear Last Bandoleros playing on Honcho's iPad. The music reminds me of the night we met Alice, the friendly server at the All-Night Truck Stop in Bentonville, Arkansas. She told us her oldest brother found work out west that the Bixby Mine began running a second shift, and they needed workers. Millie and I were so excited we took turns driving over a day and a half straight through to get there. When we showed up on a Monday morning, Mr. Blake, a stocky man in his late fifties, hired me to work on the second shift and asked Millie if she wanted to earn some extra money.

My first shift started that afternoon with safety training, and Millie would start work on Wednesday. We both were sure things were finally turning around.

Mom watched Bobby while we worked. Mr. Blake learned we lived out of our car and decided to give Millie an advance on her pay. He even took time to help her find a place for us while I worked. After we moved in, everyone had their own space and privacy. Even our old cat got comfortable enough to wander out from his safe place in the back window. I knew we were heading in the right direction, and a better life was around the corner.

About two weeks later, Millie met me on the porch when I came home from work. I approached to hug her, but she backed away.

"Everything okay?" I asked. "You don't want a hug because I'm wearing my work clothes?"

"It's not you." She stroked her soft hand against my cheek. "I'm fixing burgers, so get cleaned up."

"How was your work today?" She paused without looking back.

"I didn't go." She didn't appear sick, but she didn't look right either.

"What's wrong?" She blinked repeatedly but wouldn't face me." What did you tell Mr. Blake?"

She shot a tearful glare back at me. "I don't want to talk about it." She was weeping as she went inside.

I tried not to be upset, but we needed the money. I thought it best not to push it; I figured it must be one of those female things she needed to sort out. After all, we had a lot of change going on, and I was thankful we had a place to stay. Besides, Mom would be with her, and when she got ready, we would work it out, no matter what. Things were going to work out fine, and I knew it.

The next afternoon, me and old 201 took off for the mine, feeling pretty good about the new place until I saw Mr. Blake waiting for me by the time clock.

"Stewart, would you step into my office, please?" I could tell something was up by his tone of voice.

"Sure thing, Mr. Blake."

"How do you and the Misses like working here?" His posture stiffened as he motioned for me to take a seat.

"We like it fine, Sir. Why do you ask?"

"I've been disappointed that Millie, mind you, I like her work, but, well, I think you should talk with her."

"Disappointed about what?" I asked.

He paused, looked off to the side, and stroked his mustache before speaking. "It's her attitude. She's been absent for two days now, and that won't do. We all need to work as a family around here, and sometimes we gotta do extra things to get along if you catch my drift."

"Sure, I'll talk to her when I get home," I remember answering as my mind was screaming, this is serious.

Usually, time flies when loading heavy ore deep below; but that night time stalled. The mine seemed smaller, the walls seemed closer, and the jackhammers louder. Even the stale air one hundred feet below was harder to breathe. Logic told me Millie needed to work at least until her Mom's disability check came to cover the rent we owed. I had a sense of dread, but my heart told me to trust Millie's judgment.

At quitting time, I wash my hands and splash my face in preparation to rejoin civilization. Mr. Blake's office messenger enters the locker room and hands me an envelope. My heartbeat thumps in my throat. The ringing in my ears blocks the jeering of my co-workers. Everyone is watching as I open the envelope.

"They want me to work overtime. Ole Man Blake signed the authorization himself!"

"What did you promise to give?" one asked.

"What do you mean?"

"Blake doesn't do favors without getting something in return."

Why did they say that about him? Didn't he give us jobs, help us get a place, and advance the rent money?

Millie was again waiting for me on the front porch when I got home. I got out of the taxi, sprinted to the porch, and slid in next to her on the swing. Her eyes were reddened as if she had been crying.

"Doing any better, Honey?" I asked.

"Maybe we should think about moving on."

"How can you say such a thing when we are starting to see our way clear." I bang my palms on the porch railing and unfold the note. "I just got approved for overtime, and you want to move on?" She sat with her hands folded in her lap. Her almond eyes, the ones that owned my heart from the first meeting, told me she was troubled and deserved my support.

"Have you talked to your mother about this?"

"Well, sort of," she said.

"What's that supposed to mean? Sort of?" She grabbed her shawl and went into the house. Mom came to the door to let Norman out.

"Mom, what's wrong with Millie? I'm doing my best to keep everybody happy, except I can't please her anymore. What am I supposed to do?"

Mom listened patiently and occasionally nodded, letting me know I had her attention without ever volunteering anything that may show favor to me or Millie. I guess whatever Millie was going through, she was doing her best to keep it to herself.

A thin woman bumps against my shoulder startles me back to the reality of picking beets. She struggles to carry a loaded basket.

KINDNESS WITHOUT SPEAKING

"Here, let me help you." I reach out to her. She nods from under a ragged straw hat for me to step back to let her pass by. "Okay, I get it."

I understand why she may think I need help more than her. How odd must I appear to her? Why would an uncoordinated white man, throbbing in pain, be trying to offer her aid when she does this scorching fieldwork for a living?

Pulling beets and dragging the baskets gets more challenging as the sun moves directly overhead. I wonder how my family is doing with little water and if the blanket gives them enough shade. Our cat is the only one I'm sure can take care of himself.

A horn repeatedly honks for the harvesters to stop work and make their way toward the barn. I stumble after them, the fragrant aroma of spicy food floats through the air. Women gather cold drinks and load plates for the harvester's lunch break. Today will only be a rest break for me, but tomorrow, me and my family will have plenty to eat.

I scan the lot for a shady place to slump against the baskets near the barn. I squat and lean back to lay my head against my palms.

"?Donde esta su comida?" a deep voice calls out. I raise my head to look; Honcho is staring at me, frowning with his hands resting on his hips.

"Am I not supposed to sit here?" I ask.

"He wants to know where your lunch is." A child with long black hair stands before me, using her hand to shade her dark brown eyes from the bright sunlight.

"Hi, who are you?"

She glares at me, then shifts, placing her hands on her hips. "I'm Carmelita, and he's waiting for an answer."

"Oh. I see. Well, I'm not eating lunch today because I need to diet for a while." I hope the lie didn't show in my eyes.

Honcho shakes his head, takes hold of the girl's hand, and walks away without a word. I lean back to close my eyes. The language is different, but the food aroma and happy sounds around me remind me of the farmer's market back home. What I would give to be there now, eating barbecue and corn on the cob.

"Hey, Mister." The child's voice brings me back to reality. The little girl approaches me holding out a coffee can. With each step, water sloshes over the brim onto her outstretched arms.

"Here, use this to wash." The little girl hands me a paper towel and pours water over it. I can't remember anything more soothing than splashing this water on my face and letting its coolness trickle down my neck. I let some flow over my head as she gives me another towel.

After my wash, Honcho peels open a tin foil pouch so large it covers both of his palms. The fragrance of warm tortillas, combined with the aromas of the pork roast smothered in garlic, hot peppers, and tomatoes, astound me. He stands before me, holding this heavenly bounty of food. For the first time today, my mouth is moist. I am drooling like a wild animal.

Honcho's face is void of expression as he gives me the bundle and mumbles instructions to the girl.

"It's for you to eat so you can do work! No good if you can't work!" she says.

"Is he your daddy?" I ask.

"Yes, and he's the boss." Carmelita wraps her arms around his leg. "So, you'd better eat."

I can't believe these people care enough to give me food. A lump swells in my throat. I'm so thankful for their generosity that my voice becomes shaky.

Honcho hands her a bundle. She plops on a basket nearby, tears off a tortilla chunk to use as a scoop to pick up the beans. She nods for me to try it. I inhale the rising steam and give a silent prayer of thankfulness. Honcho watches as Carmelita shows me how tortillas make scoops to **eat** with. I tear a tortilla to scoop it into the meat; the taste bursts with the flavor of fresh-baked Italian bread topped with shreds of spicy tomato garlic meat. Both relief and guilt wash over me--my desire to share this with my family claws at my insides.

My aching body rejoices from the delicious food while my mind questions how I could ever repay these people for sharing what little they have. I look up from the bundle of food and bow my head to show appreciation of their kindness.

The horn again signals it is time to return to the field. I finish the water can and wrap the leftovers to take with me. As I try to get up, my back doesn't want to let me walk upright anymore. Many of the passing workers notice my stiffness and smile as I limp back into the glare of the midday sun.

By two o'clock, my shirt drips with sweat, and my mouth is dry --every pore in my body itches from the dust off the field. We will be safe if I can hold on till dusk; I'll get paid. The bright sky finally eases into a softer pinkish-blue, announcing the day will soon surrender to evening. What a wonderful word, "evening," The end of a workday, and I will then be able to rescue my family.

Honcho checks my baskets before loading them on the flatbeds. He tallies my day's work with a partial smile and nods for me to join the line of workers washing up by the barn. It looks as if washing after work is a ceremonial rite of passage. The first person holds the bucket for the next in line to wash and rinse. As I get closer, I see that the other workers have sores on their hands and scratches on their forearms too.

The others also have holes in their faded clothing. Even in this condition, men wear gold chains while women wear gold in their pierced ears. Does moving from place-to-place cause them to trust gold more than cash?

THE PAY LINE

Workers stand in a single-file line with their straw hats held to their chests before passing in front of Honcho's wooden crate desk. He pulls a wad of cash from his pocket, lays it out in stacks under the flickering light from a kerosene lantern. Each worker gives a slight bow of respect after receiving his or her wages.

My turn comes as the last loaded flatbed rumbles out from the lot. Honcho looks up at me while tilting his head to the side to keep the cigarette smoke away from his eyes. He points to the blisters and scrapes on my fingers and laughs. His cigarette falls into his lap, and he jerks back to flick away the embers. The jolt knocks over the crate. Stacks of bills fall, and the lantern spills its flame onto the ground. I laugh as he scrambles to regain his position. The night becomes deadly silent. Only the whisper of a breeze and the wail of a far-off creature fill the void.

He grabs the money and lunges at me with an outstretched hand going for my throat. Twisting my collar, he knots my shirt up under my chin and lifts me onto my tiptoes. Droplets of saliva fly as he yells. I am not sure what he is saying, but I am positive he is not someone you laugh about. Trembling before him, with only my toes touching the ground, "I'm sorry... I didn't know." I raise my arms with palms showing forward.

Slowly he lets me down to erect the crate while keeping one eye on my every move. He finally let go while counting out $40.00, but when I try to pick it up, I see him pulling something out from his back pocket. Chills go up to my spine as my body stiffens. Is he going to shoot me? Am I going to die here? I'm too weak to fight and too exhausted to run. With a head bob, he tosses me a pair of worker gloves. I almost wet myself as I catch them. As the others did, I bow and say thank you. As I start to move on, he snaps his fingers as he points at the money in my hand. I hold it out to him, and he plucks six dollars back like a chicken pecking a June bug. Somehow, just eye contact, we both understand these gloves are worth more.

Nighttime brings a lively spirit to the barn lot. Sparks rise as women stirs kettle over the campfires while the men laugh and share drinks from a bottle. The cooking aroma drifting from the camp brings my taste buds to attention and reminds me of how hungry my family must be. I approach a toothless elderly woman adding branches to her fire. Fortunately, she understands the gestures I'm making when I point to her kettle and then to my money.

I trade her part of my wages for tamales from a steaming pot and a coffee can filled with spicy chicken and rice. She gives me a plastic bag of fluffy warm tortillas to go with a container of refried beans. Buying home-cooked food for my family energizes me and lifts my spirit. The leftover twenty-four dollars goes back into my pocket for future needs, and I head out to feed my family.

About a mile away from the taxi, the moon gives an eerie glow, and I get the feeling something is wrong. Even the raised arms of the Saguaros appear as tormented souls, trying to warn me. I adjust my hold on the food packages and limp into a staggering jog. Thumping pulses in my ears after a few yards as coyotes howl in the distance.

SOMETHING'S WRONG

The flickering amber glow of the dome light of the Checker tells me I'm almost there.

"Is that you, Stewart?" Millie hurries to meet me. She wipes the sweat from my face and confesses she was relieved to hear my footsteps. Her touch is clumsy and tense.

"What's wrong? Is Bobby, okay?" I ask.

"It's Mom! She has been sick all day and is getting worse. What are we going to do?" Millie slumps into my arms, crying as she blurts out, "I'm scared. Mom doesn't look good at all."

"It's okay. We'll get through this," I say

Millie takes my hand and leads me to where Mom is resting in the back seat.

"What is it, Mom? Is it the heat?" I ask. She didn't answer; her eyes have a fixed milk-glaze stare.

"How are you feeling, Mom?" I ask in a louder voice this time. She continues to stare off without acknowledging.

"She's burning up with fever."

Bobby tugs at Millie's sleeve. "Is grandma, okay?" She cradles his cheeks in her palms and looks directly into his eyes.

"Yes, Bobby. Grandma needs to rest." Millie sobs the words and dabs at her eyes. "Why don't you go see what Norman is doing?" She kisses him on the forehead and turns him away.

"Wait, I brought water." I give a cup to Bobby and one to Millie. "See if Mom will drink some. There's food in here too." I open the sack to show her. "Try to get her to drink while I go for help." Tears stream down Millie's face.

Bobby rubs his eyes and snuggles under her arm. "Go ahead and eat without me. I'll be back with help as soon as I can."

I take off down the road to get help; my legs are numb when I reach the basket barn. The smell of food and coffee lingers in the air. Workers sit around a campfire, swap stories, and laugh. Sparks rise into the endless night sky as a man stokes the fire with a stick.

"Does anybody here speak English?" The laughter dies down; the man with the stick drops it and turns toward me. "Mom is sick, and we need help!" I say. "Please, can anybody understand me?" The barn lot falls silent except for the campfire crackling.

"Over here!" a familiar-sounding voice said. I turn around to find Carmelita leading two women out of the darkness. "Tell me. They will help you."

I bend down to be at eye level with her. "Mom is sick- high fever has set in, and she is not responding." Carmelita translates my words to the women. They exchange glances of concern, and they rush back into the darkness.

"Where are they going?"

"No worry, they'll get what they need," she said.

Moments later, the campfire reflects off their shining faces as they return. One has her arms full of bags, towels, and jugs of water; the other calls for Honcho. He gets a truck started while Carmelita runs to the kettle near the fire for hot water. I help the women climb onto the truck bed.

As we hurry along this road, the reflective mile markers appear to extend endlessly into the blackness. "Why couldn't the taxi have broken down someplace closer to civilization?" The weight of my responsibility mounts with each minute. I should have known better than to leave Mom in the desert this long.

On arrival, the women make sweeping gestures ordering everybody out of their way. One sets out to make herbal tea while the other tends to Mom. Even though I can't understand what they say, I know that they are concerned. The younger of the two helps Mom take sips of hot tea. The other takes Mom's clothes, piles them on the hood, and grabs towels and a jug of water.

Carmelita speaks with them and tells us they cover Mom in wet towels to break her fever.

"They say it's a stroke from too much heat." Carmelita nods her head as if in agreement with the diagnosis. "They make her comfortable now and want us all to pray she gets better."

The women extend the sign of the cross as a blessing on us before leaving.

Millie opens the packages I brought and rolls meat and refried beans into tortillas like Taco Bell does. She offers one to me. "You and my boy go first."

Bobby smiles at the taste of his cup of chicken and rice. "Mama, you cook good!"

"That's because you're such a good eater." She kisses his cheek.

After he finishes eating, Millie puts Bobby down in the front seat for the night. Neither of us has much appetite, but I take a few bites upon her insistence. With the comfort of the food and my folding chair outside by the campfire, I submit myself to the beautiful seductress of dreamless sleep.

THE NEXT DAY

The faint odor of cigarette smoke wakes me just before seven o'clock. Millie is backing her way out of the rear seat.

"Is Mom better?"

"She's a bit stronger, but she still looks awful." Taking a deep breath, she looks around. "Do you smell that?"

"Yes, smells like someone is smoking."

I peek around the fender, and to my surprise, I come face to face with Honcho. He smiles as he gets up to dust himself off. I guess he spent all night on watch in case we needed more help. Coming up the road, Carmelita leads workers bringing food and fresh coffee. Following them is a rusty truck driven by an elderly man with a wiry white beard. The brakes screech as it creeps close to the taxi's bumper. The driver attempts to cram the limp shift lever into reverse, but the gears won't engage. As the gears crunch, the engine sputters, the truck lurches back against the bumper. Four-letter-sounding expletives erupt from the toothless driver. Women to blush shout for him to stop, and cover their ears.

"What's going on?" I ask Carmelita.

"You can't stay here." She spoke her words with her arms folded like an authority. "We are taking you home with us." My heart pounded as if it would burst out of my chest. My mind searches for answers; why are they doing this? What do they want from us?

Mom wasn't fully awake when the workers hooked a log chain to the front bumper of the Checker. We gather the blanket, and all get inside and secure the doors. Gears grind, and smoke spews from the exhaust. The elderly man moves his truck forward and watches over his shoulder as he takes up the slack in the chain. The Checker lurches and moans as it rolls out of the sand.

"What's happening?" Mom rises up.

"It's okay. We are moving to a safer place," Millie says.

"Yeah, Grandma, A whole bunch of people came to help," Bobby stands, pointing his arm out the window.

I steer as they tow us away from the godforsaken desert, three miles until we are in the shade behind the basket barn.

This side of the barn has a different atmosphere than the other side where the trucks park. It has hanging laundry, crying babies, bubbling open pots of chicken soup, and skillet goods nestled near the campfire embers to bake. The sights, aromas, and sounds open my breathing and make my heart glow with excitement -- so many people in such a crowded space. Everything is like a honeycomb of bees caring for each other.

The Checker comes to rest as the flatbed gently nudges us against the barn. With the cracked block, I know this will be the taxi's final journey, but it is a fresh new start for my family. Norman springs out of the back window to investigate the noises and smells. He zips into the barn with his head low and crooked tail high as if on a hunting expedition. Many curious little faces, several missing front teeth, gather to see inside the Checker.

"We are gonna need something for the windows." Millie rolls her eyes.

"I'll rip the blanket into pieces to cover the glass."

The women who helped us so much last night knock on the top of the car to enter.

One holds a steaming cup of chicken broth as the other raises Mom to get a spoonful down. Neither Millie nor I understand what they are saying, but Mom's puckered expression fades away, and she asks for more. The caregiver's eyes sparkle with delight. Millie pulls at my shirt to hug me.

"Carmelita, who are these nice ladies?"

"This is aunt Juanita and aunt Rosaria. They are sisters." She grins.

"Both are your Aunts?"

"Of course, Almost everybody that works here is an aunt, uncle, or cousin. We stay together so that we can help each other. That's what families do,"

"Will you thank them for us?" I ask.

"Okay, I tell them." She claps her hands as she bounces on her toes. "THANK YOU!"

We all laugh at how a ten-year-old has such a keen understanding of life. The women finish, wave goodbye to us, and back away.

"It's time for me to go to work. You all should be okay here, and if anything comes up, I am nearby," I give Millie the money from yesterday and put on my gloves.

"Don't worry about us," she nervously glances around her. "We'll be fine. I'll get more food, and we'll have lunch waiting for you. Go on now."

A NEW START

Today the sun is out, but my mind is more at ease. The sprinkler heads are shutting down, and the air carries the fragrance of spring rain. Flatbeds rumble past the end of each row to drop off baskets. The ground is moist, and my new gloves protect my hands from the crisp leaves. Straddling the first beet, I bend over with a thankful heart that yesterday's trials are behind me. I yank. Even the beets seem to be more cooperative.

I worked my row all morning, keeping pace with the others. My high stack of filled baskets gives me pride. Hissing irrigation heads begin to spew water--dark-eyed children hold baskets above their heads and dare each other to run through the spray. Children shriek and giggle as the cool droplets fall on them. Standing here brings back happy memories of worry-free children playing back home. Of course, that was before the company sold our town out to foreigners.

The deeper I dive into my work; the faster time goes by. It will be lunchtime in a couple of hours and I'll eat with my family and celebrate the gift of security that this work provides.

I don't think about Millie's reasons for leaving Tucson in the coming days. Even though we don't have abundant opportunities here, this place may work out for us. My boy enjoys playing with new friends, and Mom is on the mend from her stroke. Juanita and Rosaria let Millie help clean baskets to earn money. Even old Norman now has a steady job chasing mice in the barn.

Harvest season always ends, and migrant workers have to move on. Today, I sold the tires and transmission, the last usable parts from the taxi, for seventy-five dollars. I hated to do it, but the money will help buy food until we find work again.

"What do you think about us moving to San Diego?" I ask. Millie stares at the horizon and runs her fingers through her hair as if in deep thought.

"We don't know anybody in San Diego, do we?"

"I know. But if we could get a job at Sea World?"

" Sea World!" Carmelita waves her arms and rushes over with a sparkle in her eyes. "My Grandma has a restaurant near there."

"In San Diego?"

"Yep. We go there to help her until next crop." She swivels on her heel as if dancing. "You can ride with us." Bobby's eyes fill with anticipation; Millie nods her approval with a glance.

"You need to ask your father, just to be sure," I say.

Carmelita's pigtails fly as she runs to find her father. Thinking about moving on is exciting but brings back the fear of being alone again. The notion that we may never again see these families that shared with us. Bobby speaks a second language, and Mom knows how to make tortillas, awesome burritos, and does a fair job with refried beans. I wipe my forehead on my sleeve.

"Being here was good, and our life is changing again." Millie takes my hand and leans her head against my chest.

"Let's go. There's plenty of work in San Diego; we'll both find jobs, I'm sure of it." She squeezes my hand and stretches up on her tiptoes to kiss me.

MOVING ON

Over the next few days, workers are preparing to move on. Juanita gives Mom a religious pendant as a going-away present. Her sister, Rosaria, brings us food with a blessing for our safety.

"Adios, mis amigos," they said in harmony.

"Thank you for all that you have done for us." Millie tearfully embraced them.

"Wait! These are for you angels that saved me," Mom gives the sisters handkerchiefs she made with angels embroidered on them.

The harvester community is absent of sounds of children playing and the aroma of spicy food cooking; today, they pack baskets of bedding, load cages of chickens, and noisy pink piglets. Their dogs anxiously pace by the running boards.

It is time for me to make my way to the barn door to wave the final goodbye. The old flatbeds shudder as they drive off. One at a time, gears whining, the slow procession works its way through the gate and down the road. A piece of my heart goes with each flatbed. This goodbye, the final separation from a caring community, aches in my chest.

The sun is setting, and Honcho's truck is the last to leave. We load all our belongings and tie them down with ropes to secure them. Norman makes himself comfortable to ride in the back window of the truck's cab. "C'mon." Millie yells, "Everybody else is gone." Once I'm onboard, Honcho starts the motor, flips on the lights, and drives toward the gate.

Three shiny pickups roar into the lot, blocking us from leaving. A portly man, wearing faded bib overalls, jumps out to stand in front of us. Others, eight in all, gather around him. His pink jowls puff out of his open neck shirt as he takes a drink of courage from the half-pint of I.W. Harper from his hip pocket.

"Get out of the truck," he barks. One of the others kicks at the door. "We got some things to talk about." His gaze darts to check behind him, "Ain't that right, boys?"

Before I can tell them Honcho doesn't understand English, he steps off the running board and takes a stance like a gunfighter in a western movie.

"Where's the rest of your friends, Poncho?" I jump down from the truck bed and run to the front. The look on Honcho's face is the same as when I had laughed at him. He strikes a match on his belt buckle and cups his hands to protect the flame as he lights a cigarette without taking his eyes off the men.

"He doesn't speak English."

One in the mob yelled back, "Stay out of this, boy . . . ain't none of your concern." The little man returns to his truck, bends low to reach under the seat.

"Bud, what the hell are you doing?" From the crowd, a tall clean-shaven man tugs at Bud's arm but can not stop him.

Bud straightens, wipes his face with his forearm as glints of light glance off a blue steel revolver. Mom and Millie quickly grab Bobby to hide below the dashboard.

The men move closer to circle Honcho. I try to push my way in, but one of them shoves me backward and holds me against the driver's fender. "You best stay back if you don't want to get hurt," the man said.

"Millie, hurry, get Mom and Bobby out of here." The three slide out from the passenger door unnoticed. They start to run when I see Carmelita drop to her knees in prayer.

"Quick! Get her out of here too."

Bud takes another drink, wipes his mouth on his shirtsleeve, and hands the bottle to a man on his left. His voice is raspy as the whiskey burns down his throat, "We're gonna teach you thieving, lazy, no accounts a lesson about coming here and stealing jobs."

"What jobs have they taken?" I ask.

Bud's glassy-eyed stare fixes on me. "Why boy, don't you know what's going on here? Are you blind? These lowlifes have been taking the food right out from your family's mouth!" Another man polishes off the half-pint and throws the bottle at the flatbed. **It** shatters against the windshield, leaving a spider web of cracks across the driver's side.

"Yea! That's right! They come here illegally. Then they take away our jobs," a bearded man with tattoos shakes his fist in the air. "We only want what's coming to us, and we're here to set an example for future job-stealers to remember."

I twist and tug, trying to get free. "This man hasn't done anything to you!"

Bud turns to me. "Son, you'd better stay put; this ain't nothing you need to be involved with. Hell, he wouldn't lift a finger to help you." He pushes his finger hard against my chest. I smack his hand away, but two men grab me to force me back to the truck. I look over my shoulder and see the bearded man slam a bat against Honcho's neck. Bud stood, centered in the headlights, grinning. The others have worried expressions at the sound of bones in Honcho's left wrist snapping under his fallen body. His eyes close, the cigarette he lit dangles loosely from his bruised lips.

Bud signals for the mob to rush in. One grabs at Honcho's billfold. Another raises his leg to pull off his boot. They take his smokes, sunglasses, and the belt with the silver buckle.

My reflexes freeze as my chest tightens like being in the jaws of a vise.

"Why are they doing this?" The ragged words cascade from my mouth as Honcho lies unconscious on the ground, no longer the big man. I've got to help him, but how? Seeing him through my tears, helpless, twisted, and distorted. How could he defend himself against so many?

The mob circle like wolves around a downed animal. They kick his side, spit on him, and take whatever they want. I pray for this to stop. "God. Why this man? He's done nothing wrong."

"Let's just shoot the bastard and get the hell out of here," a man yells.

Bud's eyes ignite with delight. His shaky hand aims the revolver at Honcho. The hammer clicks into position. My breathing quickens, and my knees quiver. Honcho is on the ground, so helpless and so alone. I push my body against the truck and kick at the man on the right with all my strength. He lets go of me to grab his leg. I jerk my arms free and shove my way through the mob. Without stopping to think, I lunge with all my might into Bud's gut, pushing him to the ground. His eyes fill with fear as he gasps for breath. Bud squirms and scoots on his backside, trying to get away. His trembling hand is pointing the gun at me.

"*BANG!*"

A flash of heat and gritty smoke force me backward as a white-hot poker zips into my chest and out through my back. I grab my shoulder to see if it is still attached as I stumble over Honcho's body.

"Bud! Are you crazy? You shot the wrong son-of-a-bitch! Now they'll come looking for us, sure as hell."

"C'mon, Let's get out of here." The men scamper for their pickups to speed away.

My sight is dimming, but I hear Millie scream, "What have they done? Oh! My God, Stewart!"

The dust from the pickups speeding away settles in my eyes. Millie strokes my cheeks as her hot tears drip onto my face.

"Please, somebody, help us?" I hear Bobby sobbing in the background.

"Please, bring my boy closer,"

"Quick, come to daddy,"

My body goes limp as if I'm leaving it. Is this death? Someone is struggling to lift me. I open my eyes and see Honcho looking down at me. His lips are moving, but I can't hear. We are close, yet he appears to be moving away. I blink again and strain to clear my vision. Is this Honcho or my father holding me? My dad died years ago.

"Dad. How did you get here?" A tear rolls down dad's distorted face. He doesn't answer; a metallic taste comes up in the back of my throat as my awareness fades. Honcho stuffs his bandanna into the oozing wound as he and Millie lift my body onto the flatbed. Millie steers the truck while Honcho works the pedals. Together, they drive into town, with Mom and Bobby holding on to me.

A few minutes later, they pull into a filling station. Millie jumps out and runs to the door. "Help! My husband has been shot."

One of the men at the station yells to the attendant while pointing to a church. "Call Doc Sally to meet us over at his office, and hurry." Two others lift me to rush across the road.

"In here!" A gray-haired man in a lab coat rushes out and motions for the men to hurry. "Take him through." They carry me up the church steps into a converted medical office. It is hard for me to see where I'm at. It's as if I'm above looking down at me on a table.

The doctor orders everyone, except Millie, to leave the exam room as he snaps on latex gloves and cuts away my shirt. He straps monitoring devices to my arm and a plastic oxygen mask over my mouth and nose. "How did this happen?"

"We tried to go, but a bunch of drunken men stopped us" -- Millie's words fade into mumbling. Doc Sally notices her hands are shaking uncontrollably. He calls for Emma, his assistant, while he examines the wound.

"Let Emma help you," he says.

Emma enters; without looking up, Doc points his bloody finger in the direction of Millie and then to a chair. Emma swings the chair around for Millie to take a seat facing her.

"We need some information. Please take whatever time you need." She moves a box of tissues closer to Millie." Can you tell me how this happened?"

"He was only trying to help." Millie tugged on Emma's arm as if searching for understanding. "They wouldn't listen to reason . . . they came to kill somebody."

The doctor sent a signal with a quick movement of his eyes, glancing in the direction of the door.

"Come with me. Let's get you some water." Emma supports Millie's forearm to assist her in walking to the waiting area.

Millie took a seat next to Mom while Bobby sat on a pew across the creaky wooden floor. They overhear Emma calling the Sheriff's office to report the shooting.

HONCHO LEAVES

Outside, Honcho tries to pinch the corner of a towel in his teeth to rip it into strips to make a splint. Wincing from the pain, he calls for Carmelita to help him. She rips it over the sharp edge of the license plate. Her smiling father rests a crate board against the shifting lever to support his broken arm. He shows her how to wrap the strips around his arm to secure it to the board.

"Mejor?" She asks, rubbing his shoulder.

Long strands of her hair comb back into place as he smooths them with his fingers. "Si. Mucho mejor, gracias,"

Honcho tucks his splinted arm into his shirt and reaches for a cigarette. They were gone. He fumbles in the glove box until his hand stops; smiling, he pulls out a wrinkled cigarette. After blowing off the dust, he puts it between his swollen lips and looks in the rearview mirror to confirm the gold tooth is still there. Striking a match on the dashboard, he gazes at the fledgling flame until it becomes a bright orange. The cigarette smoke drifts out of the taxi into the desert air as Mom unloads their belongings.

Carmelita opens the passenger door just enough so Norman can get out. The cat leaps to the porch and takes a post there as if standing guard.

"Adios Mi Amigos." Honcho salutes in the direction of the exam room. As he turns the key to start the motor, he nudges Carmelita to check her door. The old truck emits smoke, and gears scrape with each shift. Mom holds back, showing her fear as the image gets smaller as it makes its way south on the road out of town. Sparkles of moonlight dance off Carmelita's dark eyes as she peeks through the back glass. Tears fall as the outline of her extended family fades away.

Back inside Doc Sally's office, Millie asks, "Is he going to be okay?" Her fingers clasped in prayer while searching Doc's face for reassurance.

"I won't lie to you; it's not good." Doc takes her hand and leads her to sit by Bobby.

"He's lost lots of blood and needs life-support that I don't have."

"What does that mean?"

"He needs your prayers. His vital signs are holding but weak. The medication should keep him comfortable for tonight." Doc stood with his back to her as he hung his white coat by the door. "We've done all we can, for now. Go home, get some rest, and will talk in the morning."

"I can't leave him like this. Besides, everything we have is in those boxes by your door." Her lips quivered as tears began to flow. "We have no place to go. We're homeless."

Doc circles the room in deep thought until he takes a seat behind his desk. He removes and slides his stethoscope in the top drawer with trembling hands. As he starts to speak, a clanging bell at the railroad crossing drowns his voice. Millie's limbs stiffen at the air horn blast; panic overtakes her. A faint scream is all the energy she has left. Her fingernails dig into the sofa arms, attempting to wake her from this nightmare. The floor of the office vibrates as the speeding train flashes past. The bell stops, Doc checks his watch and stands with his thumbs resting under his belt.

"Okay then, the restroom is through that door, and there is an empty exam table in the other room. Perhaps you can all make do here tonight. I'll check back as needed."

Mom puts exam linen over the couch and sponge bathes Bobby in the sink. To allow Millie privacy in the other room, Mom loosened her bra, then backs away to doze in Doc's chair. She turns on a light and does her best to comfort Bobby as he snuggles in for the night.

Millie prays for a miracle. At daybreak, she looks behind the door; Stewart's breathing was ragged but in tune with the blinking lights on the equipment. In the next room, she found Bobby asleep and Mom sorting items in one of the boxes.

"You need to eat something. Gotta keep up your strength." Mom offers Millie some shredded cheese wrapped in a tortilla.

"I can't. Give it to Bobby."

The beeping of the monitor stops, and both rooms go dark. A faint glow of a streetlight outlines Doc Sally as he rushes out of Stewart's room. "We've lost power, and he's not stable!"

Doc dials 911. Wide-eyed with palms against his temples, he gives the address and Stewart's vital information. "Yes, yes, I'm a doctor, I know. I've already inserted a tube to relieve his pneumothorax. I understand -- but you must hurry."

THRUST INTO THE UNKNOWN

Millie chews on her fingernails while pacing in circles. The wail of a far-off siren draws closer; red and blue lights flash in front of Doc's office as it stops.

"He needs to go now," Doc says.

"We have no way to pay for this!"

"You go with Stewart. Bobby and I'll be right here when you get back," Mom motions for Millie it will be okay.

"Slowdown," Doc stops Millie's pacing. "You're all going with him." Bobby slides off the couch and runs to open the door.

EMTs hurry in, dragging a gurney with medical equipment on it. Millie's body shakes as she pleads for answers.

"We don't have money for this." She brushes her hair away from her swollen eyes and tear-reddened cheeks. "What's going to happen to us?"

A sedan pulls in beside the ambulance. The trunk pops open as a young woman wearing a business suit hops out from the driver's side.

The EMTs in the other room count one, two, three; Stewart exhales a loud groan as if in pain. "What are they doing to him?" Doc Sally blocks Millie's attempt to rush into the exam room.

"He needs you to be strong. Gather your belongings and go with the social worker."

"Social worker? Why is there a social worker?" Millie's face goes pale, she slumps against the wall, and her eyes flutter. Doc supports her balance until the social worker enters.

"Miss Jacobson will help you get through this." His brow line furrows; he nods towards the door for Mom and Bobbie to gather their belongings and get into the waiting sedan.

Miss Jacobson walks with Millie to the passenger seat as EMTs lift the gurney into the back of the ambulance.

"Watch out for your head as you get in."

The lights flash, the doors slam shut, and the siren blares as the ambulance races away. "Buckle up and hold on." The sedan accelerates to catch up with the speeding ambulance.

"Hello, is everyone ready?" The voice comes from the dash speaker. The display on the dash screen flips to a man in uniform sitting behind a desk.

"Who's that?" Millie asks.

"We're connected to the Sheriff via video conference. He needs to ask you some questions."

Bobby waves to drivers that pull off the road to let us pass like royalty in a fast-moving parade. Millie gives the Sheriff descriptions of the suspects and details of the shooting.

"They all had 'Home of the Free' written on the back glass of their trucks."

"Thanks, We will get on this; I'll let you know what we find." The screen flips blank, then back to the map showing a blue dot heading toward Las Vegas.

"Can you get kids' programs on that TV?" Bobby pulls himself up between the seats.

Miss Jacobson glances back at him in the rearview mirror, smiles, and shakes her head.

"Sorry, No. It is not a very good TV, is it?" Bobby frowns, rubs his eyes, and snuggles back into his grandma's side without answering.

Mom dozes as the sedan speeds through the desert. Forty minutes later, Miss Jacobson turns in at the emergency entrance at General Hospital. The sudden stop and the sound of the hospital doors opening jolt her awake. EMTs slide Stewart's gurney out of the ambulance as masked and gloved medical staff rushes to escort him inside.

"This way, please." Miss Jacobson directs Millie and her family to follow her into a consultation room. Millie hesitates as she watches the gurney until the medical team disappears behind 'staff-only' doors. Bobby strains to look over the lobby railing at the colorful toys in the children's play area. On the overhead flat screen, singing children hold hands while dancing around a yellow figure with an orange beak. Bobby's backside begins swaying to the music. Mom motions for Millie to go ahead while she takes Bobby into the play area.

"What's going to happen now?" Millie darts her vision from side to side, looking for anything familiar in this strange place.

"I know this is all happening so fast, but your husband is in good hands, and they are working with him," Miss Jacobson said.

"Is he going to get better? I can't go on without him."

"Please take a seat. Here's what I know; he's on a ventilator right now. They need to improve his oxygen level before surgery, which may take up to three hours. We have to wait here to get his condition reports." Miss Jacobson tilts her head as she touches Millie's shoulder. "You okay with that? Millie slides onto a bench and holds her head with her palms. "To save time later, let's take a look into the rest of your family's needs."

"Sure, but this is all so confusing." Millie shuts her eyes while, in her mind, unanswered questions crunch against each other like ice cubes in a blender. She raises and backs against the coffee counter to grasp the edge, trying to regain her balance over her trembling. "I expected the cops to get involved." She reaches for a napkin with one hand while holding tight to the counter with her other." We're strangers here. We have no money." She glances at Bobby in the play area. "My son is playing with toys we could never afford. Why is this all happening?"

"You have been through a lot, and I know this has to be confusing. Someone told Mr. DeMarco what happened."

"The only people we know are the harvest workers, and they have moved on."

Miss Jacobson glances at her cell phone messages. "It says here your husband was shot while trying to save another man's life. Someone reported this and his bravery to the company."

Millie steps away from the counter, trying to read the message on the tablet screen.

"Honcho?"

"Hmmm, no mention of a Honcho. The report shows the caller was a child." She holds the phone up for Millie to see the text.

"Carmelita!" Millie's words gush out in uncontrollable weeping. She clasps her hands and looks up. "Thank you, dear God."

"Mr. DeMarco heard what your husband did and wants to help."

"Who's Mr. DeMarco?"

"He's the man who owns the beet fields. When locals intimidate his workers, it causes delays and increases costs."

"But, the harvest season is already over."

"Let's put it another way; he wants to help your family because of Stewart's bravery. Also, an arrest and conviction, in this case, will help to stop this from happening again."

Her cell phone buzzes. "Excuse me; I need to take this." Miss Jacobson moves away and places her elbow on the windowsill to hold her phone next to her ear as she looks across the parking lot.

"Hello Sheriff, yes, I'm with them now." She pauses a moment to look back at Millie talking with Mom. "Right, I'm sure they will be glad to hear that. Goodbye."

"Is everything alright?" Mom steadies Millie's stance. "What did he say?"

"The officers brought eight suspects in for questioning. Bud is still on the loose."

"He's the one that started it all. "Millie bumps on the chair arm with her fist.

"I know you are hurting, but for now, we have to focus on finding a place for your family to stay."

Day turns into night. Family Services books Mom and Bobby into a nearby motel while Millie props up pillows in a green vinyl recliner next to the air-conditioning in the ICU. She thumbs through the pages of a fashion magazine, looking at pictures of fashion models with perfect hair and perfect teeth. She checks her ragged fingernails, lets out a sigh, and drops the magazine to the floor.

The circles of light in the parking lot below dim as the murmur of conversations in the hallway fall off to whispers. Cool air coming from the ceiling vent is like the fall breeze back in Tennessee. Back home, where we stood naked in the basement shower on the concrete floor, massaging shampoo into each other's hair -- the soothing sensations of a slippery caress tugging against me. Millie tips her head back, closes her eyes, and inhales the fragrant aroma of memories from a gentler time.

RECOVERY

A few hours later, a voice calls. "Sorry to wake you, Ma'am; but, the doctor is on his way." A blurred outline of a woman in a blue uniform holding a cup of coffee for Millie wakes her. "Do you need cream or sugar?" Millie sits up straight, rubs her squinting eyes, and turns away from the sunlight pouring through the blinds.

"Neither. How is Stewart -- is he okay?"

"The doctor will go over that with you." The nurse steadied the coffee cup.

"He twitches and moans as if trying to speak. Can you do something for him? I think he's in pain." Millie's dark eyes flash as she pleads with the nurse.

"This medication keeps the pain away, but it doesn't block the nightmares. Look, the monitors tell the story." Millie slid her hand down Stewart's arm while watching the lines on the monitor pulsate as Stewart's chest rises and falls.

"What time is it?"

"It 6:45. Here is Dr. Romero." Millie rolled her head from side to side and pushed her fingers through her long hair attempting to untangle it.

"Hello, I'm Dr. Romero." The words came behind her as a clean-shaven middle-aged man with his flaring white lab coat entered the room. "We've been monitoring your husband all night, and he's doing as well as can be expected."

"He groans and flinches as if in pain."

"Don't let occasional groaning and restlessness disturb you. They are good signs that he's coming around."

The doctor recorded a brief note and instructed the nurse on medications. "We're hoping to try him on a liquid diet soon." He nodded toward Nurse Hansen, "She'll keep you posted, okay?"

"Yes, thank you."

Warm fingers take my hand. A tickle of surprise and delight charge as my fingers tightened around hers. Hot tears drip onto my cheek as she leans over the bed rail to kiss me.

Two days after moving me to a regular room, Miss Johnson knocks at the door as Dr. Romero hands me a menu. "You got your choice. Baked chicken with mashed potatoes or pasta covered with chicken cream sauce."

"How about fire-roasted pork with refried beans?"

"Sure, Like that's going to happen." Dr. Romero's cell phone beeps. He waves over the back of his head as he rushes out. "Enjoy the chicken."

Miss Jacobson tells me she has good news. "The Sheriff took Bud into custody this morning."

"Great!" Even though it hurts, I rise onto my elbows as best I can. "Where did they find him?"

"Strange." Miss Jacobson taps her tablet screen with her finger to enlarge the font. "It says here; they found him tied to the bumper of a wrecked pickup with a basket over his head." Miss Jacobson shrugs her shoulders as if trying to understand. "The suspect, Bud, has a broken arm, swollen lip, and his shoes and belt are missing. Who would do something like that?"

Millie's eyes sparkle with delight as she spreads her fingers over her mouth and turns away to keep from laughing. Mom's cheeks puff out as she offers a bright colored crayon to Bobby. Her glance signals Millie not to comment. I lay back to snuggle into the pillow and pretend I don't know either.

A GLIMMER OF HOPE

Miss Jacobson checks in on us almost every day to take note of how my physical therapy is coming along,

"Hey, look at me. I'm able to stand without support." Her expression seems happy to see my progress but also one of concern.

Miss Jacobson backs into a chair, grabs her tablet, and crosses one knee over her other. "What are your plans now?" she asks.

"I guess we'll have to go home." My words feel hollow. Even with Mom's disability check, we won't have enough to get by if we stay here, barely enough to get back home.

"Back to Tennessee?" Millie raises her arms to the side, glancing wildly between Miss Jacobson and me. "There's nothing to go back to."

"What else is there?" I ease back to sit on the edge of the bed.

"This might help." Miss Jacobson unfolds a formal-looking letter printed on DeMarco Foods stationary. "Says here, they want you to work for them."

"Me?" I grab ahold of the bed frame with both hands to steady myself. "You're kidding."

"Nope, since you are a hard worker, and your past references speak well of you, they are offering you a job."

"I don't understand." My mind spins with questions. "I can't harvest beets or load baskets like this. What do they want me to do?"

"It looks like a warehouse inventory clerk until you fully recover. Then, a chance at either driver or machine operator."

"Where is it?" Millie asks.

"At their industrial warehouse in San Diego." Miss Jacobson hands me the letter. "There is a note at the bottom."

Along with the job offer is a hand written note telling me DeMarco Personnel mailed a copy to a restaurant in Baja, Mexico. I can't pronounce the restaurant's name, but deep inside, I know who it is.

THE END

ABOUT THE AUTHOR

John was born in the Midwest. He loves writing, oil painting, pipe organ building, and antique car shows.

His career spans thirty years of executive positions in the financial industry, President of his business consulting company, and as an adjunct professor at Baker University,

He attended Rockhurst University, in Kansas City, where was awarded a EMBA degree. He has also earned numerous certificates for creative writing from Wesleyan University,

His work has appeared in Best Times magazine, The Benton County Guide, The Missouri Poetry Society, and numerous anthologies.

Books by him include; *The Hedgepath Ghost, Famous Pies for the Mayor's Party, Seymour's First Day at School, Jerry, the Tock-Tick Clock, and Benny's Bump.*

Books available at amazon.com/author/johnedavis

Made in the USA
Coppell, TX
01 August 2022